Princess Ponies

A Dream Come True

Princess Ponies
A Dream Come True

CHLOE RYDER

SCHOLASTIC INC.

First published in Great Britain in March 2013 by Bloomsbury Publishing Plc

ISBN 978-0-545-86072-7

12 11 10 9 8 7 6 5 4 3 2 1   15 16 17 18 19 20/0

Printed in China   68

This edition first printing, September 2015

With special thanks to Julie Sykes

The Pony

Queen
Moonshine

Princess
Crystal

Princess
Cloud

Princess
Stardust

Princess
Honey

Royal Family

King
Firestar

Prince
Jet

Prince
Comet

Prince
Storm

Cloud
Forest

Volcano

Wild Forest

Stableside
Castle

Chevalia

N
W — E
S

Horseshoe Hills

Savannah

Grasslands

Canter's
Prep School

The Fields

Mane Street

Early one morning, just before dawn, two ponies stood in an ancient court-yard, looking sadly at a stone wall.

"In all my life this wall has never been empty. I can't believe that the horse-shoes have been taken—and just before Midsummer Day too," said the stallion.

He was a handsome animal—a copper-colored pony, with strong legs and bright eyes, dressed in a royal red sash.

The mare was a dainty yet majestic palomino with a golden coat and a pure white tail that fell to the ground like a waterfall.

She whinnied softly. "We don't have much time to find them all."

With growing sadness the two ponies watched the night fade away and the sun rise. When the first ray of sunlight spread into the courtyard it lit up the wall, showing the imprints where the golden horseshoes should have been hanging.

"Midsummer Day is the longest day of the year," said the stallion quietly. "It's the time when our ancient horse-shoes must renew their magical energy. If the horseshoes are still missing in eight days, then by nightfall on the eighth day, their magic will fade and our beautiful island will be no more."

Sighing heavily, he touched his nose to his queen's.

"Only a miracle can save us now," he said.

The queen dipped her head, the diamonds on her crown sparkling in the early morning light.

"Have faith," she said gently. "I sense that a miracle is coming."

Chapter 1

Pippa MacDonald blinked sleepily and stared around the unfamiliar room. For a moment she didn't know where she was. She remembered going on vacation to the beach with her family, but this wasn't their vacation home. The bed next to hers was huge, with a straw blanket and a horseshoe-shaped head-board decorated with ribbons. And fast asleep in the big bed was a pony—a princess pony!

5

All at once Pippa's memory flooded back. She *had* been on vacation, until two enormous seahorses had whisked her away to the island of Chevalia, a magical world filled with talking ponies, where no human had ever set foot before. Time existed in a bubble there, and Pippa wouldn't be missed at home, for no time was passing in her own world.

There she'd met Princess Stardust, and learned that Chevalia was in great danger. Eight golden, magical horseshoes used to hang on an ancient wall in the castle courtyard. Once a year, on Midsummer Day, the horseshoes' energy was renewed by the sun. But the horseshoes were missing, and if they weren't returned by Midsummer Day, Chevalia would be gone.

Pippa had been amazed to learn that she'd been brought to Chevalia to find the magical horseshoes. Yesterday, after a long, exciting, and danger- ous search, she and her new friend, Princess Stardust, had rescued one horseshoe from the foothills of the spooky Volcano. But there were still seven more to find and there were only five days left until Midsummer.

Quickly, Pippa got up and looked for her clothes. She'd hung them on a chair the night before, but now in their place was a new outfit—a white top covered in pink and blue horseshoes, a pair of pink jodhpurs, and some matching sandals. Thrilled, Pippa put the new clothes on, then borrowed one of Stardust's combs to untangle her dark, wavy hair.

Stardust was still fast asleep.

"Wake up, lazy hooves," Pippa said, gently shaking her.

Princess Stardust opened her eyes, yawned, and closed them again.

"There's no time for sleeping in," said Pippa. "Chevalia is still in danger."

"I was having the most wonderful dream," mumbled Stardust. "I had a pet girl." Her eyes flew open and she sat up. "It was true!" she exclaimed. "I really do have a . . ."

Pippa scowled and crossed her arms over her chest.

"I mean, a new special friend," said Stardust hurriedly. "Today's a very special day—we should get ready."

Stardust went to her dressing table and combed her long, white mane. Then Pippa placed Stardust's pink jeweled tiara onto her head, between her ears. Pippa smiled

as she adjusted the sparkling tiara into place.

"Let's get going then," Stardust said excitedly.

Stardust's room was at the top of the eighth tower in Stableside Castle. They hurried down the tower's spiral ramp to the ground floor. They were just heading toward the dining room for breakfast when Stardust's big sister Princess Crystal appeared, going in the opposite direction.

Crystal had an apricot-colored coat with an inky-black mane and tail and a white blaze running down her face. She was extremely pretty and spent many hours making sure she looked her best.

"Hurry up," she whinnied impatiently. "There's a family meeting in the courtyard."

"A family meeting about what?" Pippa whispered to Stardust.

"We're always having family meetings," she said. "I'm starving—are you? What about breakfast?" she called after Crystal.

"You should have thought about that when you were sleeping in. It's a good thing you're not going to be queen one day." With that, Crystal trotted ahead, toward the courtyard.

Pippa put her hand on Stardust's side.

"Don't mind her," she said. "Big sisters just don't understand."

11

"She still treats me like I'm a foal," said Stardust.

"She may have a bigger tiara," Pippa said, smiling, "but you have a girl for a best friend."

"Yes, I do," Stardust said, smiling back and following her sister.

Reaching the wooden door that opened onto the courtyard, Crystal stopped and turned around. "It's Royal Family only," she said importantly. "Your pet should wait here."

"Pippa's my best friend and she's here to save Chevalia," said Stardust. "That makes her the same as family!"

Crystal rolled her eyes. "You make me tired," she neighed, leading the way.

Stardust and Pippa joined the Royal

Ponies gathered in the courtyard. Crystal and Prince Jet stood at attention, nudging each other for the best position to greet their mom and dad. Prince Comet had his nose buried in a book. Honey was doing twirls to show off her glittery new hoof polish, while Cloud was mumbling grumpily. Prince Storm strode in last, covered in mud, causing Crystal to snort angrily.

"Storm, you could have washed. You look like you just trotted off the farm!"

"I did," he replied. "The fields won't plow themselves."

"Stop bickering, children," scolded Mrs. Steeplechase, the royal nanny. She pushed the Royal Ponies into an orderly line, ready to welcome the king and

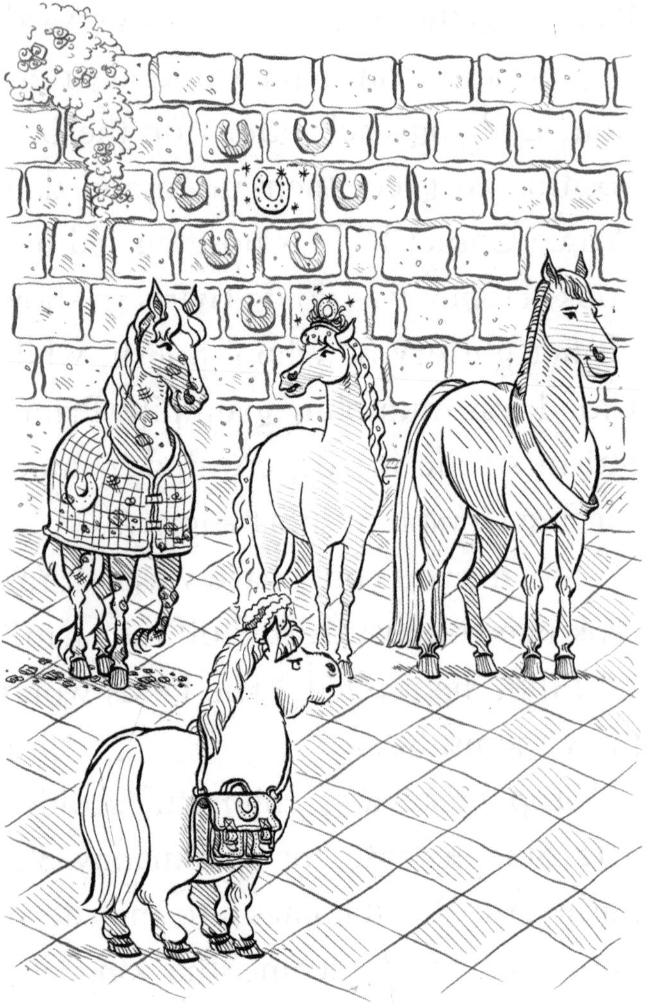

queen. "I trust you've all had breakfast and are ready for the Royal Games?"

Pippa's stomach rumbled noisily as she looked at Stardust in alarm.

"Games?" she asked. "But I thought we were going to search for the missing horseshoes."

"Was that your stomach, Princess Stardust?" Mrs. Steeplechase asked angrily. Dipping her head inside her satchel, she brought out a shiny red apple and tossed it to Stardust, who caught it in her mouth. She threw another apple to Pippa.

"Thank you," Stardust and Pippa said.

"Hmmph!" snorted Mrs. Steeple-chase. "Just don't be late for breakfast again."

Pippa stared at the stone wall, where one lonely golden horseshoe sparkled in the sunlight. There were still seven empty spaces left to fill. Suddenly she didn't feel so hungry anymore.

Stardust followed Pippa's gaze to the Whispering Wall.

"The Royal Games are very important—" she started, but she was interrupted as the queen and king trotted regally into the courtyard.

As one, the Royal Ponies straightened up, with their ears held forward. Bowing their heads, they whinnied, "Good morning, Mother. Good morning, Father."

The queen looked up at the wall and then turned to address her children. "The annual Royal Games are taking place today, and although Chevalia is in danger, it's important that we keep up our traditions. The whole island will be looking to us for how to behave. If we panic about the missing horseshoes, then everyone will panic. Do you understand?"

The Royal Ponies nodded and chorused, "Yes, Mother."

"Stardust," Pippa whispered, "if the Royal Games are so important, maybe I should look for the horseshoes on my own."

"Don't do that," said Stardust. "You'll miss out on the fun. There are so many great events—dressage, show jumping, horseshoe-tossing, polo, and the

Equestriathon race around the entire island!"

"The Games do sound amazing," said Pippa.

"They take place on the Fields," explained Stardust, "on the far side of Mane Street. It's not too far from the beaches, so we can search them afterward."

"Okay," Pippa said, feeling a little happier that Stardust wasn't completely forgetting about the horseshoes. "We'll stick together."

"Like best friends," said Stardust.

"Like best friends," Pippa agreed, stroking Stardust's long, soft mane.

Queen Moonshine whispered something into her husband's ear, then turned and nodded at Pippa.

18

Pippa flushed and her stomach did a cartwheel. She could guess what the queen had said. The Royal Ponies and the ponies of Chevalia were depending on her.

"We *will* find the missing horse-shoes," Pippa said determinedly.

Chapter 2

Queen Moonshine lined her family up in age order. Princess Crystal was first, perfectly groomed and dressed in her best tiara, looking every bit the queen-in-training. She was followed by her three brothers and three sisters, with Stardust, the youngest Royal Pony, at the end.

"What a fuss," Storm said quietly. "I don't know why I have to go to the

Royal Games when there's so much to do on the farm before the harvest."

"But the polo team needs you," said Stardust. "You're their best player."

"Do you play polo, Stardust?" asked Pippa.

"I wish I could play, but Mrs. Steeplechase won't let me. She says I'm too young." She sighed. "The only game they let me play is horseshoe tossing, which is for babies."

The king and queen led the Royal Family from Stableside Castle to the Fields at a smart trot. Pippa was glad that Mrs. Steeplechase had allowed her to ride on Stardust's back or she might not have kept up. Pippa looked out for the missing horseshoes as she rode toward the

Royal Games grounds. Away to her left was the Wild Forest. She was surprised to see that three ponies were gathered by the edge of the trees. The largest, a stocky pony, was cloaked in a dark-gray coat and hood, with a few strands of chestnut mane showing. There was something familiar about it.

"Stardust," Pippa whispered urgently, "who's that over there by the Wild Forest?"

"Where?" asked Stardust.

"Right there," Pippa said, pointing. But when she looked again, the ponies had disappeared into the woods.

"Was it the wild ponies? They're lots of fun. I wish I was allowed to play with them," Stardust said.

Pippa fell silent. They hadn't looked like wild ponies and Pippa was sure she'd seen the large, hooded animal before. If only she could remember where.

As they approached the Royal Games grounds, the delicious smells of warm bran mash and steamed carrot juice drifted toward Pippa. An enormous horseshoe arch marked the entrance. It was decorated with red, blue, yellow, green, pink, and purple ribbons that fluttered colorfully in the light breeze. One by one, the Royal Family ducked under the horseshoe arch, to the excited hoof-stamping of the hundreds of

gathered ponies. The queen led them into the royal box, which was higher than the rest of the audience and gave an excellent view of the entire show ring.

Knowing that the whole crowd could see her, Pippa carefully slid off Stardust's back. There was a loud crackle followed by a shrill whinny, then a deep voice sounded over the loudspeaker.

"Ponies and foals, please show your appreciation for the arrival of Their Majesties Queen Moonshine, King Firestar, and the Prince and Princess Ponies: Crystal, Jet, Cloud, Honey, Comet, Storm, and—not forgetting the little foal of the family—Stardust. Plus our very special guest, Pippa MacDonald."

There was a thunderous roar and the ground shook with even more stamping. Pippa's face felt hot and her chest tightened as she stared shyly at the enormous crowd. She'd never seen so many ponies all in one place. There was every kind, from tiny Shetlands with shaggy manes covering their eyes to magnificent thoroughbreds with highly polished coats.

"Mmm, can you smell that carrot juice?" said Stardust. "I could drink a whole trough of it."

"You're only hungry because you slept through breakfast," Cloud said irritably.

"I could drink a troughful of carrot juice too," said Honey. "Let's go and get some together. Do you like my hooves by the way? I wasn't sure which color to paint them."

"I *love* your hooves," said Stardust.

"They are pretty," Pippa said, taking in Honey's glittery pink-and-purple-striped hooves.

"Where did you get the polish from?" asked Stardust.

"The Mane Street Salon. Excuse me!" Honey said angrily, as Crystal and Jet pushed past to get to the front of the royal box.

"Out of my way, Jet. The crowds are here to see me," said Crystal.

"No, they're not," Jet said, winking at a group of young fillies and grinning when they blushed. "It's me they're here for."

"Well, they're certainly not here for me," Storm said, smiling at Pippa.

"I'm not surprised," Crystal said moodily. "You might have cleaned up your hooves at least, Storm, before coming to stand in the royal box."

"Don't worry, Storm," Stardust whispered. "No one's interested in me either."

Pippa sighed. Stardust seemed to have forgotten they had an important job to do.

"I'm going to start looking for the horseshoes," Pippa said impatiently.

"Wait for me! Sorry, Honey, I've got to go," added Stardust. She hurried after Pippa, stepping out of the royal box and into the crowd.

"We'll never find anything here. There are too many ponies around!" Pippa worried. Then she thought of something. "Do you think the crowd would help us?"

"That's a great idea!" said Stardust.

Stardust's excitement was contagious, and she soon had a group of eager ponies helping her to search the show ground. Pippa tried asking for their help too, but most of the ponies just stared at her in awe. They had never seen a real live girl before. In the end she gave up asking and searched alone, keeping her head down to avoid all the curious stares.

The dressage competition started and many of the ponies lost interest in searching for the horseshoes and trotted over to the arena to watch. The Royal Family was settled in the royal box, enjoying the Games. Honey had a large bag of roasted nuts that Stardust kept looking at longingly.

"Let's go and watch the dressage for a bit," she said at last, when she couldn't resist any longer.

"We can't," said Pippa. "There are only five days left until Midsummer."

Stardust nuzzled her nose in Pippa's dark, wavy hair.

"I know," she said softly. "But you heard what Mom said about the Royal Ponies needing to act normally. Let's search for a bit longer and then we really have to go and watch some of the events."

Among the trees at the edge of the show ground was a temporary stable block for the competitors. It was packed with ponies combing their manes and painting their hooves. Sashes and tail bandages fluttered from the trees and there was a strong smell of hoof oil.

31

A flash of light caught Pippa's eye. It was coming from a hollow in a wizened old tree. Something shiny was hidden inside. Her heart quickened as she went toward the light and pulled out the shiny object.

"It's just a hoof pick," she said, her shoulders sagging with disappointment.

"That's my lucky hoof pick!" said an excited voice. "At least, I hope it's lucky."

Pippa turned around to see a solid, chestnut pony, with a neatly braided mane tied with blue ribbons, trotting up behind her.

"Blossom!" Stardust whinnied, blowing through her nostrils at the pony.

Blossom blew back, giggling as they touched noses.

"Are you competing in the junior dressage?" asked Stardust.

"I can't get out of it," Blossom said sadly. "You will come and watch me, won't you? Pleeeeease! I know I'll mess it all up if my best friend isn't there to cheer me on."

"I'll try," Stardust said. "But Pippa

and I are busy right now. Pippa's here to find the missing horseshoes and I'm helping her."

A hurt look crossed Blossom's face, but she swallowed and said bravely, "I know. Everyone's talking about her—a real live girl here on Chevalia."

"She's my best pet ever," Stardust said proudly.

Pippa rolled her eyes and cleared her throat, hoping that Stardust would remember that she wasn't a pet.

"I mean, Pippa's my best friend," Stardust said quickly, realizing her mistake.

Pippa noticed that Blossom's big brown eyes glittered with tears.

"B-b-best friend?" she stuttered. "I thought I was your best friend."

"You are. Well, you were until Pippa arrived," Stardust said. She did not see that Blossom was sad. "Pippa's my best friend now, but you can be my second best."

Just then the announcer called for the start of the junior dressage competition.

"Listen—they're calling your class," said Stardust. "You'd better go."

"So are you coming to watch me?"

"I'm sorry, Blossom, but Pippa and I—"

"We'd love to watch," Pippa interrupted. "We'll both cheer you on!"

Pippa felt very uncomfortable as

they followed Blossom to the competition arena. It was obvious to her that Blossom was upset, but Stardust didn't seem to have noticed.

"Blossom's too clumsy to be any good at dressage," Stardust whispered. "It's too bad, because she comes from a family of show ponies."

When it was Blossom's turn to perform, she trotted stiffly into the ring. Her hooves were all over the place and she kept tripping up.

Cinders, an unkind pony who was always quick to criticize others, was in the box below the royal one. She laughed as Blossom stumbled around the ring.

"Blossom's got four left hooves,"

she whinnied. Some of the other ponies laughed and snorted with her.

That only made Blossom worse. She trotted around the show arena like a circus clown. She finished with a shaky curtsy and hurried from the ring in tears.

"What's wrong with her?" asked Stardust. "She always does badly in dressage, so why is she crying about it now?"

"Blossom's crying because you said she wasn't your best friend anymore," Pippa said quietly.

"That's silly!" Stardust exclaimed. "We can still be friends, but how can I have two best ones?"

"Very easily," said Pippa. "It's good to

have lots of friends. Imagine how you'd feel if I suddenly said I wanted to be Blossom's best friend and not yours."

Stardust's face fell. "I thought you liked me!"

"I do, but that doesn't mean I can't like anyone else. I've got another best friend at home."

"But you like me at the same time?"

Pippa nodded.

"Oh, I see," Stardust said slowly. "You *can* have two best friends."

Now that the junior dressage was over, Pippa wanted to continue searching for the missing horseshoes but she didn't want Blossom to be so upset, especially when it was partly her fault. She decided to hide her impatience

39

because she knew they had something to do first.

"Let's go find Blossom and tell her she can be your best friend too," Pippa said.

Stardust looked unsure. Pippa climbed onto her back and stroked Stardust's mane.

"Having two best friends will be twice as much fun," Pippa promised.

"Okay," said Stardust. "I will have two best friends. Let's go and tell Blossom."

Chapter 3

At first Stardust and Pippa couldn't find Blossom. They searched everywhere, including the competitors' area, but there was no trace of her. Then Stardust spotted her on the far edge of the show ground.

"Blossom's going the wrong way!" she said. "That path leads down to the beach."

"She's fast!" Pippa exclaimed, watching Blossom gallop into the distance.

Blossom galloped all the way down the path and didn't stop until she reached the beach. Stardust was hot and panting heavily by the time they caught up with her. Blossom stood staring out to sea with the surf swirling around her legs.

"Hi, Blossom," Stardust said breathlessly. "You can still be my best friend if you want. Pippa says I can have two."

Pippa slid from Stardust's back and glared at her. "Say sorry," she mouthed silently.

Stardust tossed her head as if she might argue, but Pippa kept glaring at her.

"I'm sorry," she said at last. "I didn't mean to hurt your feelings."

"Really?" Blossom continued to gaze at the sea.

"Yes," Stardust said, giving her a friendly nudge with her nose.

Finally, Blossom turned around. "So we're still friends?" she asked.

"*Best friends*," said Stardust. "It's going to be twice as much fun having two best friends."

"Can I be friends too?" Pippa asked, looking at Blossom.

"Yes! A real live girl for a friend would be amazing," said Blossom. "I'm sorry I ran away. I was upset, and when Cinders laughed at my awful dressage performance it was the last straw. I try so hard but I always trip over my hooves."

"You're great at galloping," Pippa said kindly. "You should enter the Equestriathon."

"I'd love to, but Mom and Dad think that racing is for any old pony, not show ponies like us." Blossom sighed.

"Traditionally Blossom's family has always been a family of prize show ponies on Chevalia," added Stardust.

"She can't just decide to be a racing pony."

"But we can't all be good at the same things," said Pippa. "My mom says you should do the things that make you happy."

"Well . . ." Blossom paused. "I do love to gallop—it's my favorite thing. Well, that and being Stardust's best friend."

"Pippa's right," said Stardust. "You should do the things that make you happy. And even if you don't win the trophy, every pony that finishes the race gets a medal. But I'm sure you *can* win!"

Blossom fell silent for a while, then she said bravely, "I'll do it. I'll race in the Equestriathon. And if I win the trophy, hopefully Mom and Dad will be so proud of me they won't mind about the dressage. Will you come and support me?"

"Of course," said Stardust.

Pippa bit back her frustration. She couldn't hurt Blossom's feelings by refusing, but she was worried that at this rate they'd never find the missing horseshoes.

"Thank you." Blossom's eyes sparkled happily. "And one more thing, now that we're all best friends—can Pippa ride me in the Equestriathon? Pleeeeease! You know how much I've always wanted to carry a girl."

"That's a great idea, isn't it, Pippa?" said Stardust.

Pippa hesitated. "Won't you run faster without me, though?" she asked.

Blossom's bottom lip quivered.

Pippa didn't like seeing her upset again, so she quickly added, "How about I just ride you to the start line?"

"That would be wonderful! Thank you, Pippa. We'd better get going. I need to warm up on the practice gallops."

As Blossom and Stardust trotted back up the beach, Pippa trailed behind, kicking up lumps of seaweed and checking behind rocks for the missing horseshoes.

When they reached the path toward the Fields, she turned back for one last look. Something caught her eye away in the distance. Pippa squinted out to sea and her heart missed a beat. It was Rosella and Triton, the two giant seahorses who had brought her to Chevalia. She wondered if they would be able to help. Pippa ran straight back to the water's edge, waving to get their attention. Gracefully, the seahorses changed direction and swam toward her.

"Hello, Pippa," the pink seahorse named Rosella called.

"Is there a problem?" asked Triton, a green seahorse with dark freckles.

"Yes," Pippa said breathlessly. "Princess Stardust and I have only found one of the golden horseshoes."

"Only one?" exclaimed Rosella. Pippa noticed that the seahorses gave each other disappointed looks.

"We brought you here, Pippa, because you are the girl who loves ponies the most," said Triton. "We hoped you could save Chevalia."

Pippa felt awful. "I won't let you down," she promised, "but I could use your help."

"What help do you need?" asked Rosella.

"Could you swim around the island and look at the places we can't see or reach from the land, like the rocks?"

"If there are horseshoes on the cliffs or in the rocks underwater, we'll find them," said Triton.

"Thank you," Pippa said gratefully.

Proudly dipping their heads, they swam back out to sea.

Pippa raced to catch up with Stardust and Blossom. The two ponies were so busy talking about how Blossom should compete in the Equestriathon that they hadn't even noticed she'd been gone.

While Blossom warmed up for the race on the practice gallops, Pippa searched the ground on either side of the racetrack for horseshoes. She wasn't surprised when she didn't find them, though—it was too open and flat to hide anything there.

At last it was time to ride Blossom over to the Equestriathon start line on the beach. A long blue ribbon marked the start of the race and a huge crowd had gathered all along the track. As Blossom approached it, proudly carrying Pippa on her back, the ponies began to whisper and stare. Pippa's face burned with embarrassment when she realized they were talking about her.

"Carrying a girl is cheating," said a large pony with a narrow face.

"It's not fair to the others," agreed an elderly black-and-white pony.

Pippa was very glad when Blossom reached her position on the start line. Sliding from her back, she stood close to Stardust, hoping the princess pony could protect her from the mean looks. Once she was off Blossom's back,

everyone returned their attention to the competitors.

"Good luck, Blossom!" Stardust shouted, earning herself a glare from Mrs. Steeplechase, who was also in the crowd. "Once you've started, we'll go to the cliffs to watch the rest of the race."

"Thank you," Blossom said, looking pleased. "I couldn't do this alone."

King Firestar stepped forward. "One hoof, two hooves, GO!" he called, striking a horseshoe-shaped gong.

The blue start-line ribbon fell to the ground. In a thunder of hooves and flying turf, the competitors galloped away. Blossom kept pace with even the

biggest and most powerful of the racing ponies.

"Quick, Pippa," said Stardust. "Jump on my back so we can get to the cliffs faster. It's the best place to watch from because you can see at least half the race from there."

As soon as Pippa had swung herself

onto Stardust's back, the pony set off at a gallop across the Fields. The wind blew in Pippa's face, catching her wavy hair so that it streamed out behind her. She felt her worries slowly melt away. This was thrilling—the most fantastic ride in her whole life. She wanted to gallop forever. Leaning forward, she sank her hands deep in Stardust's soft, white mane.

"Faster," she cried.

Stardust snorted. "Hold on tight then," she called, pushing onward.

Pippa could tell that Stardust was enjoying the ride too. Her ears were pricked forward and she galloped with a joyous spring in her stride.

Pippa was so happy she almost

Chapter 4

They reached the cliffs quickly and Stardust stopped a safe distance from the edge, her sides heaving as she caught her breath.

Pippa looked around. From this point, over half the island's white beaches were spread out below her. The island was ringed by deep-blue water that sparkled like thousands of tiny jewels. It was so quiet up here

that she could hear the soft hiss as the
waves crept up the shore. But the
beaches were a long way down and it
gave her a sudden shiver to be up so
high. She clung onto Stardust's mane
and Stardust gently moved back, sens-
ing Pippa's nervousness.

"That's much better," said Pippa.
"Chevalia's the most beautiful island
ever, but it's very, very high up in some
places!"

Pippa looked down the stretch of
beach to watch the ponies racing across
the sand. Even though they were so
tiny from this height, it was still possible to pick them out. White sand
sprayed from their hooves as they thun-
dered along. The stocky chestnut in the

lead was Blossom. In second place, and a long way behind, was a paint pony, his neck stretched and steam rising from his body as he struggled to catch up. Next there was a tight cluster of four ponies who were bumping and jostling each other as they ran. The rest of the racers were spread out behind, with a group of stragglers bringing up the rear.

"Look—Blossom's so far ahead of the pack!" said Pippa.

"No one can catch her now," Stardust whinnied. "I'm sure she'll win."

Excitement buzzed in Pippa's stomach. She couldn't wait to see Cinders's face when Blossom won the Equestriathon trophy. And what would Blossom's parents say? They might be show ponies, but Pippa felt sure they'd be thrilled and proud of their daughter.

"You can do it, Blossom!" Pippa called.

Stardust joined in, chanting, "Blossom, Blossom, Blossom!"

She trotted on the spot, bouncing Pippa up and down. It was so much fun that at first Pippa didn't notice that something was moving out at sea. Faster and faster, two shapes were swimming toward the shore, where they started dancing in the water. That got Pippa's attention. She put her hand up to shield her eyes from the sun.

"The seahorses are back," she gasped.

But what were they doing? Suddenly, Pippa realized that they must want to speak to her.

"Who are you waving at?" Stardust asked, as Pippa threw both arms in the air.

"Rosella and Triton," Pippa answered,

sliding from Stardust's back. "They're calling me."

"I'll take you down to the path to the beach," said Stardust.

Pippa hesitated. Riding Stardust would be much quicker than going by foot, but what about Blossom? They had promised to watch her race.

"Thanks, but you'd better stay here. If Blossom gallops past when we're on our way down the cliff path, she won't see you cheering her on and she'll be so disappointed."

"You're right," Stardust said with a big sigh. "Why does being a best friend have to be so difficult sometimes?"

"I don't know," said Pippa. She climbed down from Stardust's back and, stroking her softly on the nose, added, "But it's worth it."

"Definitely," Stardust agreed, nudging Pippa's hand.

"I won't be long. With any luck, I'll be back for the end of the race."

Pippa set off at a run, racing across the land as if she were in the Equestriathon herself. The ground was bumpy and covered in long, spiky grass that whipped against her legs. She gritted her teeth and ignored it. She ran so fast that she almost missed the path. Pulling up sharply, Pippa turned left and stumbled down the steep track. Stones rattled under her feet, and once she slipped and nearly fell. Throwing her arms out to save herself, she flushed hot with panic. Luckily, she regained her balance and kept going, more slowly this time.

Far away, the seahorses watched, bobbing up and down in the water so urgently that Pippa thought this must be an emergency. The path turned abruptly, catching Pippa totally unaware and causing her to trip. One minute she was running, the next she was pitching headfirst down the path. She was so shocked that her heart skipped a beat. Instinctively, she curled into a ball. She tumbled to the ground, hitting the path with a dull thud and rolling a short distance, until she stopped.

"Ouch!"

Now her heart was banging like

a crazy drum. Everything ached. Carefully, Pippa sat up and tested her arms and legs. She was amazed and relieved to discover that nothing was broken. Dusting the dirt and grit from her clothes, she took several deep breaths to steady herself, then stood up slowly.

Out at sea the seahorses seemed to be still now. Pippa waved to show that she wasn't hurt. But as she started off again, something pinged against her ankle. Stopping, she stared at her foot.

"Oh no!" Pippa said.

The strap of her sandal had snapped, leaving the shoe hanging uselessly off her foot. Pippa stared at it for a moment, then quickly tied the broken ends together. The strap wasn't long enough and kept coming undone. She pulled a crumpled tissue from her pocket and wound it around the broken strap like a bandage. But as soon as she took a step, the tissue fell away. Angrily, Pippa pulled the sandal off. Now what was she going to do?

Chapter 5

There was only one solution. Unbuckling the other sandal, Pippa slid it off, then, holding a shoe in each hand, she bravely set out again. Dust oozed between her toes and tiny stones bit into her feet. Pippa ran on, gasping with pain and hobbling each time she stepped on a really sharp stone. She was much slower without shoes, but she continued down the winding cliff path as fast as she could. She just hoped the seahorses would wait for her.

At last, the path flattened out and she could see the beach ahead. With an extra spurt of speed, Pippa ran onto the white sand, squealing with delight at the softness. Faster now, she hurtled across the beach and splashed into the sea. The water was deliciously cold and soothing to her aching feet. She waded out until the sea reached her knees.

The seahorses met her, their enormous curved tails brushing the ocean floor. Dipping their heads, they each touched their noses against Pippa's.

"Well done," Rosella said, her eyes sparkling proudly.

"You were very brave just now," added Triton, his voice gentle and deep.

Pippa flushed. She didn't feel brave— more annoyed that she'd fallen and broken her shoe.

"Have you found something?" she asked.

"I believe we have," said Triton.

Pippa's heart leaped with joy, then instantly sank as she could tell from the seahorses' nervous faces that it wasn't all good news.

"Is it a horseshoe?" she asked.

"We think so," said Rosella. "Something shiny and glittery is wedged in the rocks at the end of that jut of land. Can you see it?"

Pippa stared into the distance. She could see the rocks—three of them, with jagged tops and steep sides—but that was all. She took a step sideways and saw something flash.

"Yes," she said, her voice rising with excitement. "There's definitely something sparkly between the middle and end rocks."

"You'll have to hurry," warned Triton. "The tide has turned and very soon those rocks will be underwater."

"Once the sea comes in, it will be too late," added Rosella. "There's a nasty whirlpool around those rocks. It's very dangerous. Even with our magic we're not strong enough to get close to them."

Pippa looked at the rocks. They were so far away and the sea was rapidly creeping up them. Suddenly she felt very small and alone. Could she really do this by herself?

"I have to!" she said forcefully.

Pippa rushed along the beach. The sand was soft under her bare feet but running down the path from the cliffs had taken more out of her than she'd realized. The muscles in her legs ached with every step. She could feel herself slowing, and no matter how hard she tried, she couldn't make her legs work any faster. She knew the water was bubbling up the beach, its frothy white fingers curling around the rocks. What if the tide beat her and the whirlpool pulled the golden horseshoe loose, whisking it out to sea?

"No!" she panted. She couldn't let that happen. All eight of the golden horseshoes had to be in place on the Whispering Wall in time for Midsummer Day so that their magical energy could be renewed and Chevalia would be safe.

There was such a long way to go. It seemed hopeless, but Pippa didn't give up. On she ran, her heart pounding loudly in her ears, blocking out all other sounds. It was only when a shadow fell over her that she realized she wasn't alone.

"Stardust!" she squealed.

"You were gone such a long time I was starting to worry. I had to come and check you were okay. Get on my back," Stardust called, slowing to a walk.

"I'm so happy to see you!" exclaimed Pippa.

"Well, what are best friends for?"

Pippa stumbled alongside her. Her legs were trembling and she didn't think she had enough energy to jump onto Stardust's back. Stardust seemed to realize this because she stopped and knelt down on her front legs.

"I hope Mrs. Steeplechase isn't watching right now!" she joked.

Pippa couldn't help laughing too. The royal nanny was so strict she wouldn't care if all seven of the missing horseshoes were in danger of being swept out to sea—manners and behaving like a proper princess pony came first!

Climbing onto Stardust's back, Pippa sank her hands into her silky mane and wound it around them.

"Comfortable?"

"Very," said Pippa.

She lurched sideways as Stardust rose up, only just remembering to squeeze her legs into Stardust's sides to prevent herself from sliding over the pony's head.

"Let's go," Stardust called, bucking with excitement as she raced away.

Pippa leaned forward like a jockey, taking some of her weight from

Stardust's back as they galloped across the beach. Sand sprayed up from Stardust's hooves and her long white tail streamed behind her like a silky banner.

Was it her imagination or was the sea coming in even faster now? Pippa couldn't take her eyes off it as she willed it to slow down. It was no good. The sea closed in, licking against the bottom of the rocks and becoming deeper and deeper, until it spun around them in circles, like water whirling around a drain.

"Faster!" Pippa cried.

She threw herself flat against Stardust's neck. Stardust galloped harder, her breath coming in noisy

76

rasps. Slowly, the rocks came closer, but poor Stardust was exhausted. As the pony lost speed, Pippa could hardly watch the sea's greedy blue fingers reaching up the rocks to the glittering object wedged there.

Bravely, Stardust galloped on but her stride was shorter and she kept

stumbling. Now that they were closer, there was no doubt that the glittering object was a golden horseshoe. But there was still some distance to go to reach it. A white wave lapped over the horseshoe.

"Oh no!" groaned Pippa.

They'd finally found the second horseshoe, but any second now they were about to lose it again.

Chapter 6

A pony was thundering up behind them, neighing loudly. Was it Mrs. Steeplechase? Pippa was afraid to look. But no, surely the royal nanny was too large to gallop that fast. Turning her head, she saw that it was Blossom.

"Blossom!" exclaimed Pippa. "What are you doing here?"

"When the racecourse turned a corner I saw you both from the cliff top.

You promised you'd watch me and I knew you wouldn't let me down, so I guessed something must be wrong if you were here on the beach. What's happened?"

"We've found one of the golden horseshoes," Pippa said, pointing at the distant rocks. "But it's almost underwater!"

"You won't get there in time to retrieve it," Blossom said, galloping beside Stardust. "I'll go for you."

Relief swept through Pippa but it was quickly replaced with despair.

"What about the race? You were in the lead."

"I pulled out. Chevalia matters far more than the race." Blossom snorted.

"Besides, winning isn't everything. Helping your friends is much more important."

"But how will you get the horseshoe off the rocks?"

"With my hooves," Blossom said bravely.

Pippa shook her head. The whirlpool was already too strong. Blossom would need all four hooves on the ground to stay safe.

"I'll come with you," she declared.

"There isn't time to stop for you," called Blossom, who was starting to pull ahead of Stardust.

If Blossom was making sacrifices and putting herself in danger, then Pippa must too.

"You don't have to stop. Come closer and I'll jump on your back," she shouted.

"Pippa, no!" shouted Stardust. "It's too dangerous. And you're scared of heights."

But Pippa was too busy concentrating to answer. As Blossom moved closer, Pippa noticed that Blossom was taller than Stardust. Could she manage to jump from one pony to the other without falling off? With a shudder, she ignored the pounding sound of Stardust's and Blossom's hooves.

Blossom matched her pace to Stardust's until she was exactly alongside her, then she closed the gap between them.

"Ready?" Blossom called.

Pippa swallowed hard. She felt dizzy suddenly but there was no time to lose. She reached out for Blossom's mane. It was still braided from the dressage competition so there wasn't much for her to hold on to. And how did she think she was going to get her legs over? Pippa realized that she would have to get into a crouching position to jump from Stardust's to Blossom's back. Pippa stared at the ground tearing by. It seemed like a very long way down.

I can't do it, said a scared little voice inside her head. But Pippa had already done so much on Chevalia that she'd never thought possible. Gathering all

her courage, she held on tightly to
Stardust's mane. She decided she would
do it on the count of three.

One, two, and . . . three.

Slowly, she leaned forward and
brought her feet up behind her, onto
Stardust's back. Seeing the ground
moving so fast beneath her made her

feel a little bit sick. Pippa refused to think about that. She fixed her gaze on Stardust's mane as she got her feet in the right position. Her heart was racing in time with Stardust's hoofbeats and her mouth was dry. Pippa took a long, deep breath. She pushed herself up so she was crouching on Stardust's back. Now all she had to do was to jump over to Blossom. Pippa reached out for Blossom's braided mane.

"I'm ready," she called.

"Be careful," shouted Stardust.

Pippa hesitated. Her head was spinning.

"Are you sure about this?" called Stardust.

Pippa didn't answer. She summoned

up every last bit of courage—and leaped!

Her stomach dipped. She seemed to hang in the air forever, but it was only a few seconds before she landed with a bump on the other pony's back. Blossom was wider than Stardust and had a much bouncier stride. Pippa was flung up and down for a moment, then, losing her balance, she slid sideways.

"Help!" she squeaked.

Pippa hung on, her legs gripping more tightly around Blossom's sides. Blossom misunderstood this movement—thinking that Pippa was asking her to go faster, she sped up. Lurching forward, Pippa desperately clung to Blossom's braids. She couldn't fall off now—there wasn't time! She pulled herself to the middle of Blossom's back. She knew that she had been very lucky that nothing had gone wrong so far. Now that she had regained her balance, Pippa leaned forward and urged Blossom on.

"Go, Blossom! Go, Pippa!" Stardust called, as Blossom galloped ahead.

Only the tops of the rocks were visible now. Blossom raced across the glistening, wet beach and into the sea, her steps slowing as the water deepened.

"Careful," Pippa said, feeling Blossom strain against the current.

"Look!" cried Blossom. "The horse-shoe!"

It was upside down, wedged between two rocks.

Just then a large wave crashed into Blossom, making her stumble.

"Eeek!" Pippa shrieked, as the wave soaked her too.

"Sorry," said Blossom.

The ocean floor was uneven and covered in slippery seaweed. Pippa was amazed at how steady Blossom was as she waded on.

"Don't ever let anyone tell you that you're clumsy," Pippa told her.

"I'm not now, am I?" Blossom said happily. "It's because I'm really concentrating and I'm not worrying that everyone is watching and laughing at me."

When they were just an arm's length away from the rocks, Blossom suddenly stopped and wavered.

"Oh, horseflies!" she exclaimed. "The current's too strong. This is as close as I can get!"

Chapter 7

Pippa stared at the rocks. Beneath her, the water swirled and bubbled like a giant's cooking pot. If she fell off Blossom trying to reach the horseshoe, she'd never be able to swim against the current.

I'm not going to fall, she told herself. But Blossom's legs were buckling against the force of the whirlpool.

"Blossom, can you stand very still while I climb up your neck?"

"Yes," said Blossom, "but hurry! The tide's coming in really fast, and I can feel the whirlpool sucking at my legs."

Pippa quickly pulled herself toward Blossom's head. She clutched Blossom's mane with one hand and leaned over to the rocks. If only she could stretch a little bit farther . . . Growing red in the face, Pippa reached out until her fingers were brushing the horseshoe. It was almost in her grasp.

Almost.

But the horseshoe was wedged firmly between the rocks and just couldn't be pulled free.

"Please hurry," Blossom said urgently.

It was no good. The task needed two hands. Pippa let go of Blossom's mane

and tried again. The horseshoe budged by the tiniest amount, then stuck tight. Carefully, Pippa wriggled it backward and forward. It reminded her of wobbling a loose tooth. She rocked the horseshoe forward and backward until it shifted a bit more.

"Hurry!" whinnied Blossom.

The water was still rising and was splashing around Pippa's bare feet now. She yanked the horseshoe as hard as she could.

Over the roar of the whirlpool, Pippa thought she could hear Stardust calling her name from the shore. It made her feel braver to know that her best friend was cheering her on.

With all her might, she pulled at the horseshoe again. She felt it scrape against the rock, then suddenly the golden horseshoe came free. The suddenness took her by surprise, and she slid backward, almost losing her balance. Wildly, Pippa grabbed Blossom's mane. As she did so, the horseshoe slipped through her fingers.

"No!" Pippa snatched at it, trapping it against Blossom's neck and only just preventing it from dropping into the churning water.

"I caught it!" she yelled.

Immediately Blossom swung around to face the beach, and then froze in her tracks. Standing in the water a few hooves away were two scruffy ponies.

"Night Mares!" Pippa gasped, recognizing Eclipse and Nightshade from the previous day and realizing that they were the ponies she had seen at the edge of the Wild Forest.

"Give that back," Eclipse said in a mean voice.

"It belongs to us," said Nightshade.

The water was rising even higher

now, and Pippa worried that they'd all be carried out to sea.

"PIPPA!" Stardust called from the shore.

Stardust's cry gave Pippa an idea.

"This horseshoe belongs on the Whispering Wall," said Pippa. Then she shouted to Stardust, "Catch!"

Pippa hurled the horseshoe into the air and Stardust galloped to catch it in her mouth.

"NO!" cried Eclipse.

"Let's get out of here," Pippa said to Blossom.

Blossom waded back toward the beach, and Pippa turned to see Nightshade and Eclipse still standing in the water, staring up at the cliffs. Pippa followed their gaze and saw the mysterious cloaked pony looking down at them. The two Night Mares were just standing, as if glued to the spot, in the rising water.

"You two!" Pippa called, as Blossom pushed farther toward the shore. "Get out of the water—it's dangerous!"

Pippa felt Blossom's muscles tighten as she bravely fought against the tide. One careful hoof at a time, she waded back to the beach. Clutching Blossom's mane tightly, Pippa cheered her on until, at last, they were back on dry sand.

"That was close," said Blossom.

"Too close," agreed Pippa.

Stardust trotted up to Blossom and Pippa and gave the horseshoe to Pippa to hold.

"I tried to call to you," she said. "Those Night Mares came out of nowhere."

"They were watching us," said Pippa. "And there was someone else watching too."

"Who?" asked Stardust.

Pippa pointed to the top of the cliff, but the cloaked pony had vanished. She then turned to check on the Night Mares in the water—they were soggy and defeated, but wading clumsily through the shallows.

"I don't know," admitted Pippa. "But I do know that we should get this horseshoe back where it belongs——on the Whispering Wall!"

Stardust darted next to Blossom and, side by side, they raced across the beach, leaving the Night Mares behind.

Pippa looked back to see the Night Mares emerge from the water. They started to come after Pippa and her friends, but the gap was too big for them to catch up. With an angry toss of their heads, they turned and galloped away in the opposite direction.

Blossom and Stardust began to climb the steep cliff path.

"You did it!" Stardust said, her dark eyes shining with happiness.

"We all did it," said Pippa. "Together!"

"I'm glad I have two best friends," said Stardust.

"Look," Blossom cried suddenly. "The giant seahorses are watching."

Pippa proudly waved the golden horseshoe above her head. The seahorses reared up in delight. Droplets of water flew from their spiky manes, falling

like silvery fountains. Pippa sighed happily as she prepared to slide from Blossom's back.

"Don't get down yet," said Blossom. "I don't feel tired now."

"What about the race?" Pippa asked. "Don't you want to go back and finish it and get a medal?"

Blossom shook her head. "There's always next year. I'll definitely enter the Equestriathon again, but right now I've got something that's much more important than a medal—two best friends."

"Best friends forever!" said Stardust.

"Forever," Pippa and Blossom agreed.

Slowly, they went back up the path, stopping to pick up Pippa's sandals.

"Oh, I don't even remember dropping them," said Pippa. "I'll have to go barefoot. They're broken."

"Don't worry, the royal blacksmith will fix them for you," said Stardust.

Excitedly, they made their way back to the Royal Games grounds on the Fields. It was impossible to keep the horseshoe a secret. When they approached the show arena, a crowd of ponies quickly gathered to greet and cheer for them. Pippa blushed deep red as some of the bolder ponies reached out to touch her with their noses as she passed.

The queen and king were in the royal box watching the end of the Equestriathon. Pippa slid from Blossom's back

as Stardust led the way in. Quick as a
flash, Cinders came out of her own
box to block Blossom from following them.

"Only members of the Royal
Court are allowed in here," she said
nastily.

But the queen had already seen that

Pippa was carrying a horseshoe and she excitedly waved Blossom in.

"It's not fair," Cinders hissed to her mother, Baroness Divine.

The baroness narrowed her eyes. "Good things come to those who wait," she whispered back.

Pippa wondered why Baroness Divine never had anything nice to say, especially now, when they'd found another of the missing horseshoes. She soon forgot the baroness, though, as she dropped a curtsy to Queen Moonshine. The queen was the most beautiful pony she'd ever seen. Her golden coat seemed to glow and her pure white tail fell elegantly to the ground.

The queen's face lit up with joy.

"The second missing horseshoe," she whinnied. "That's wonderful news. I'm very proud of you all."

King Firestar stamped his hoof in agreement. "We must put the horseshoe right back where it belongs," he said seriously.

A look of worry crossed the queen's face. "But it's almost time to award the prizes."

"Stardust and her friends have proved themselves trustworthy and reliable. They could take the horseshoe back," King Firestar suggested.

"Yes, please do," the queen replied.

Pippa was secretly pleased. There was something special about the golden horseshoe. Holding it gave her a tingling feeling that made her think the magic was rubbing off on her somehow. It gave her courage.

☆

When they reached Stableside Castle's courtyard, Pippa stood up on Blossom's back and carefully hung the

horseshoe on the ancient stone wall. The three friends stood back to admire it as it sparkled prettily in the late-afternoon sun.

"Two horseshoes are safe." Stardust sighed, staring up at them in wonder.

"Our quest isn't over yet," said Pippa. "There are still six to find."

"You've done enough for one day, child," the king said, striding into the Royal Courtyard. He was accompanied by two ponies, with gleaming chestnut coats, who Pippa didn't recognize.

"Mom and Dad!" said Blossom.

"I thought you were staying to award the prizes," Stardust said to her dad.

"When a father is proud of his daughter," said the king, "he should tell her."

"And that goes for show ponies too," boomed Blossom's dad. "You made your mom and me very proud today. We never realized how fast you were. If you want to keep racing instead of doing dressage, you have our full support."

Blossom beamed with delight. "Thank you," she whinnied.

"Now let's go back to the Games grounds," said the king. "You three deserve to have some fun—and we've got the evening's entertainment ahead."

"A banquet, dancing, and a huge fireworks display at the end," Stardust said happily.

"Oh, I love fireworks!" said Pippa.

☆

Long troughs had been put up in the main arena of the Royal Games grounds, and serving ponies were filling them with crunchy caramel apples, sugar-toasted oats, and candied carrots. Music was playing, colored disco lights were flashing, and lots of ponies were dancing together.

The three best friends ducked under the horseshoe arch, but as they started for the arena Pippa heard someone shout, "They're back!"

At once the music stopped and the disco lights went out. The dancers became still and the crowd fell silent. Pippa flushed as all eyes turned toward her, Stardust, and Blossom. The queen was in the royal box and she waved them forward.

"Your determination and courage have resulted in another horseshoe hanging back where it belongs," Queen Moonshine said in a clear voice. "The Royal Ponies and the ponies of Chevalia thank you. Blossom, you have shown yourself to be a true friend of Chevalia. By putting the island's needs before your own, you missed out on winning a prize in the Equestriathon. For your courage and true selflessness, you deserve a special award. Step forward."

Nervously, Blossom did so. The queen smiled as she placed a glittering tiara on her head. The sparkling gemstones were designed as a blue rosette, like a flower in bloom.

"To Chevalia," said the queen.

"To Chevalia," cheered everyone, with Pippa, Stardust, and Blossom cheering the loudest.